KEELY JAKES

EVERNIGHT PUBLISHING ®

www.evernightpublishing.com

Copyright© 2017

Keely Jakes

Editor: Karyn White

Cover Artist: Jay Aheer

Photography: Heather Almendarez/ HeatherLynn Portraits

ISBN: 978-1-77339-390-2

KEELY JAKES

DEDICATION

To the real James and Treat, who, by example, have me living healthier.

Special thanks to CJ's Athletics of Plano, Texas, House of Gainz of Georgetown, Texas, and Treat Training, LLC of Tyler, Texas, for their assistance in research.

KEELY JAKES

IRON LUST

Keely Jakes

Copyright © 2017

Chapter One

James Christian stalked across the parking lot, grumpy as a hungry bear after a long winter. Even the downpour of rain did nothing to cool the anger that had been growing since he'd woken up, over an hour late. His alarm clock had decided some time during the night to die, and it was the six-fifteen call from his six o'clock client that had finally roused him.

Not only had he now missed that appointment, which threw his entire schedule off, he had had to skip his own first-thing-on-waking-up fasting cardio session. This close to his next competition, he could not afford to miss any workouts.

Upon arriving at The Gym, where he met his Thursday morning clients, he found someone had parked in his space. He had been a member and trainer at The Gym since before the place had opened to the public. Everyone knew he always, always, always parked in the same space. The last space in the first row was *his* parking space. But today, with rain was coming down like a firehose had opened up over central Texas, a bright red Hummer filled the spot.

Dawg, owner of The Gym, had to be happy. Membership and actual participation had grown like an atomic mushroom cloud as word had spread through Georgetown about the new, no frills, gym.

Soaked to the skin by the time he stepped through the front door, James paused just inside the door long enough to pull the sopping wet bandana off his head and wring it out. The large, water absorbent rug on the floor soaked up the falling drops instantly. He then used the damp cloth to wipe the excess water from his face and neck. Scanning the large space that had once been a grocery store, he did not see Bea Wiggins, his seven o'clock client.

Looking to the desk, he smiled at Rosie, the morning manager. "Bea not here yet?"

Rosie shook her head and held out a slip of paper. "She called. Said she was having car trouble and rescheduled for Saturday morning."

James nodded as he took the slip. "Thanks."

Rosie's smile grew snarky. "I live to serve."

"Yeah, sure you do," James said as he headed across the weight room to the locker room.

It was a well-known secret that Rosie only worked there because she loved Dawg, and would do anything for the man. The fact that the man seemed oblivious to her feelings was also not lost on anyone who watched the two together. A closet romantic, James had decided to give his friend another couple of weeks before he took a twenty-pound kettle ball to the side of Dawg's head to wake the man up to a few basic facts of life.

If only he could find the right man to fill the emptiness in his own life. But being in the gym twelve hours a day, either training for his next competition, or working with his clients, did not leave a lot of time for romance, especially since being out of the closet gay in this business was not encouraged.

As he crossed the gym, James's nose twitched as

the scent of unwashed body sweat grew heavier. By the time he reached the locker room door, his eyes were burning from the stench. It was time to talk to Dawg, again, about buying one of those air purifying machines one of his friends suggested the last time he groused online about the problem. Just because people came here to sweat did not mean the place needed to reek of body odor.

That was just plain nasty.

Entering the men's locker room, James headed to the far back corner where his locker was located. His water-drenched clothes were sticking to him and growing colder by the second. The last thing he needed now was to catch a cold.

Turning the corner, he stopped, instantly captivated by the man dancing in the middle of the locker room. It wasn't that the man was dancing, but the fact that he wore only a jockstrap. The black elastic waistband stretched across the man's lower back while leg bands separated tree trunk-like legs from a high, tight, well-rounded ass that James would kill to possess.

The dancer's arms were equally huge. Hell, the man's entire body was perfection if James was any judge of bodybuilders, which he was, having been a trainer and bodybuilder for most of his life.

James could not help the smile that grew as the man's lily white ass twerked up and down and side to side in time with the music. So caught up in admiring the ass wiggle and bounce, James was caught off guard when the man spun and he was no longer staring at shaking bare ass, but at the face of a familiar cartoon tiger. James knew the animal because he had bought a stuffed Tigger for his nephew, William, the newest member of the Christian family, just last week.

"Oh, hey, how you doing?" the dancer said,

drawing James's fascinated gaze from his groin to his face. He had stopped dancing, but appeared not the least bit embarrassed at being caught.

James felt his cheeks burn as he raised his gaze from below the waist to the man's face. He took in short black-brown hair and bright green eyes that seemed to glow with joy. Fortunately, the song ended just then and the news came on.

Swallowing hard, James forced himself to say, "Good morning," as he circled around the man and made his way to his locker in the corner.

"I'm Treat. Treat Daniels."

"James Christian."

"I'm new here," Treat continued, as he stepped up to a locker that was a half dozen down from James's.

"Uh-huh. Who are you training with?" Though his day had been shot to shit at this point, there was no reason to take it out on the stranger. After all, he was always up for adding a new client to his roster. Especially one who might actually follow his suggestions and regimens.

"I'm not here to train, well, not *just* to train. Dawg convinced me to join the staff and train my clients here," Treat said. He pulled on a pair of loose, black shorts and a form-fitting t-shirt that had the sleeves cut off.

Forcing himself not to continue ogling the man, James turned to his own locker. After hanging his wet things in the small locker in the hopes they would dry before the end of his work day, he quickly pulled on a clean, dry t-shirt, sweatpants, and his gym sneakers. Once dressed, he slammed his locker shut then tested to make sure the lock had caught.

"So, you training or working today?" Treat asked as he followed James across the locker room.

"Both," James answered, feeling not quite as gruff as he had a few minutes before.

Something about Treat Daniels had drained away the grumpy bear mood, leaving James feeling almost aroused. Though he would never get involved with someone so obviously high maintenance and, well, immature.

"How old are you?" The question popped out of James's mouth before he had a chance to filter himself.

"Thirty-three. You?"

James did not answer. He was too busy kicking himself. At thirty-three, Treat was a decade younger, and to James that was the equivalent of cradle-robbing.

As soon as they stepped out of the locker room, James said, "Excuse me, I see my next client is here."

"Okay. We can talk later," Treat said. He did not sound the least bit offended at being put off.

His easy acceptance pricked James in the conscience. This bad mood he was in had to go and fast. He was known throughout the gym, and the rest of his life, to be laid-back, easygoing, and one client had described him as the most Zen person she had ever met. It was past time to let go of the day's shitty beginning and move on.

Stopping three steps from the locker room door, James closed his eyes and took several deep breaths, pushing down the irritation and negativity that had defined his day so far. His nose twitched at the sour scent, but he focused on pushing down the negativity and calling up calm. Once his mood rose, he opened his eyes again, and automatically scanned the gym.

Treat leaned against the check-in desk, flirting with Rosie. Even though he just stood talking, he continued bouncing up and down on the balls of his feet. The man obviously had a problem being still. But, that wasn't James's problem. Treat Daniels was too young and bouncy for James's taste. And, if the smile he was shining in Rosie's direction was anything to go by, the man wasn't even gay.

For some reason, that thought made James sigh with disappointment.

Since Bea had canceled, he had an hour before his next client. Turning toward the line of treadmills and elliptical machines, he decided to squeeze in some cardio while he waited for his next client. As he started running on the first open treadmill, he forced Treat Daniels and the fun the man could have brought into his life from his thoughts.

****

Though he'd only had five clients follow him from the last gym he had worked, Treat kept himself busy, but could not keep himself from watching James every time he had a spare minute. The man was older, maybe forty by Treat's guesstimate, but still in amazing shape.

"He's in training," Rosie said late in the afternoon while Treat was helping her collate new member paperwork at the front desk. "And when he's training for a show, there's no room in his life for dating."

Treat couldn't help his grin as he winked at the receptionist. "Who said anything about dating him? Maybe I just want to debauch him."

Rosie giggled as she shook her head. "I don't think that word means what you think it does."

Treat chuckled before he said, "Corrupt, lead astray, mess up, but in his case, it means to fuck one another until neither of us can walk a straight line."

Rosie's giggles turned into full-fledged belly laughs, which drew the attention of the handful of people in the room. "Okay, so you do know what the word means. Good luck with your debauching."

Treat looked across the gym and met James's dark brown eyes. "I'm not sure I'll need luck. I just hope he doesn't tear me limb from limb for making a pass at him."

As he spoke, his gaze locked with James's and held. Treat's smile widened at the heat he saw radiating from the other man's eyes. Then James blinked, frowned, and turned away.

"I think he might be heteroflexible. From the looks he's been sending in your direction all day, he's more than a little interested," Rosie said softly as she pulled something up on the computer. "If you want a few minutes alone, I'd suggest you head to the locker room now. Tawny is his last client on today's schedule, and they'll be finished in about five minutes."

Treat grinned and patted the woman's hand in thanks. "I think I'll just wander back and make sure the locker room's straight."

Rosie giggled once again as he sauntered away from the front desk. Treat headed across the room, forcing his eyes to stay on the locker room door and not look in James's direction. The sexy bald man was now in the open area, leading his client through a series of cooldown stretches.

Pushing into the locker room, Treat did check to make sure no one had trashed the place in the last ten minutes. Then, going to his locker, he opened it and changed into his street clothes. He didn't have any condoms or lube with him, but vowed to stop at the store and stock his bag on the way home so he would be prepared for tomorrow.

Today he would just test the waters, see if James was even interested in anything he had to offer. After watching James and more often than not finding him watching back, Treat felt like they were a pair of lions circling and sizing one another up.

Just as he began pacing the locker room in anticipation, the door opened. Treat sucked a breath as his cock, which had been semi-hard all day, surged to iron rod hardness when James walked in. Without thinking, Treat stalked across the room, stopping when only a single inch separated his body from the taller man. Placing his hands on James's hips, he forced James backward until the man was backed up to the door.

Even then, Treat did not stop. He continued forward until the soft cotton of their shirts was all that separated their bodies. James radiated damp heat, and Treat smiled when he felt James's muscles rippling against his own. Was the man fighting a need to take over and dominate him? Or was he planning to pound Treat into the cement floor?

Treat did not care, because he had a feeling if it came to a fight, they would be fairly evenly matched. The half-foot difference in height did not concern him, either. The intense heat James's dark chocolate brown eyes radiated gave him hope that James was, in fact, interested.

Sliding a hand around the back of the taller man's neck, he pulled until their lips were within easy kissing range. His conscience chose that moment to prick at him, stopping him from closing the last fraction of an inch that separated their lips.

Though James had not fought him off, he also had not reacted positively, either. He had not shoved Treat away, but with his arms hanging loose by his sides, neither was he actively participating in the embrace.

Pulling his head back until he could focus on James's entire face, he asked, "You are gay, aren't you? Oh, God, please tell me you're gay."

Chapter Two

James fought down the laughter that threatened to burst out at the desperate look in the grass-green eyes that stared into his. He forced himself to take a deep breath to calm himself. Then he licked his lips. Treat mirrored his action, and James's thickening cock jerked in response. The man really was too sexy for his own good, whether he was trying to be or not.

"I'm bi, but when working I don't discuss politics, religion, or my sexuality," James admitted softly as he shifted his hands to latch onto Treat's narrow hips. "That keeps my clients, both male and female, from hitting on me."

The relief that flooded Treat's eyes was instantaneous. "Oh, thank God."

Treat slid a hand up to wrap around the back of James's neck. Instead of pulling the man's head down to kiss him, he froze again. It seemed that, for the second time in minutes, the man was unsure of himself. He just stared into James's eyes, as if searching for something.

"What's wrong?" James asked. James was an alpha, type A kind of guy, but held back, waiting to see how far this vivacious, bouncy man would take things before he would take over.

Treat took a breath then frowned slightly. "You're not taken, are you? I don't poach. Tell me now if you're already spoken for."

James smiled. "No, Tigger, I'm not taken. I've been single for about a year now. How about you?"

"Single. Very, very single," Treat responded, sounding a little breathless.

James felt a shiver run through the man's entire body. It was past time one of them made a definitive move. Since he was the older, and probably wiser, of the two, he decided it was up to him to move things along.

Lifting a hand to mirror the hold the man had on his neck, he smiled when Treat's eyes went wide and began to burn with arousal. James slid his hand around so he could use his thumb to press Treat's jaw up, tilting his head back a bit farther. Shifting his own head to the right so their noses wouldn't smash together, James leaned down and closed the distance between them.

His lips brushed over Treat's fuller ones, but that did little to satisfy the hunger that exploded deep in his belly. So he did it again. And again.

Each touch only added fuel to the lust-driven hunger that raged in his core. He had never felt anything like it before, so deep, so fast, and he didn't even know anything about the man.

He continued placing kisses on Treat's lips, though each one grew longer in duration. Finally, James could take no more. His head shifted to the right, and he sealed their lips together. His tongue swiped across the seam of Treat's mouth before pressing for entry as his arms slipped around the smaller man's back.

He wanted to roar with joy when Treat's lips parted at the same time his arms slipped around to hold James tight. In the next instant, the kiss turned carnal in a way James had never experienced before. Lips and teeth and tongues came together, as the two men took the oral mating deeper and deeper.

James could hardly believe what was happening, but also did not have the strength to pull back and stop. From Treat's enthusiastic response, he must feel the same way. Rubbing full bodies together only added to his arousal.

He was about three seconds from tearing their clothes off and taking this further. Problem was, he didn't have a condom in his pocket and doubted Treat did, either. The rooster crowing in the silent room at the same time a vibrating started against his left hip jerked him back from the edge of insanity.

Pulling back and breaking the kiss was one of the hardest things he had ever done, another being to pull his arms from around Treat and step back. Only then did he notice he was now pressing Treat against the door instead of the other way around. When had that happened?

Taking another step back, James held a hand between them when Treat straightened as if to follow. "No, stay right there. Don't move." The order emerged in a low, rough voice he barely recognized.

Treat did not argue. Instead, the powerful man leaned back against the door before crossing impressively massive arms over his barn door-wide chest. "So, what's up?" he asked. A smirk crossed his lips as his gaze dropped down James's body, obviously taking a visual inventory.

James felt his cheeks go hot, which was unusual as nothing had embarrassed him in years. He fought the urge to drop his hands and cover the hard cock that pressed hard against the front of his pants. Instead of answering the question, he noticed that Treat's Tigger jock was apparently having a hard time containing things as well.

Swallowing hard, he took another step back. "I have an appointment and need to get going."

Hoping Treat took the hint, James turned and headed to his locker. He'd given himself a few extra minutes to change and get on the road, but those were speeding by. If he wasn't changed and out the front door of the building in the next three minutes, he would be late.

And after the way his day had started, James did not want a repeat of his morning.

"So, I guess I'll see you around," Treat said from where he remained at the door.

His dejected tone had James stop and pull out his phone. After shooting off a quick text to let his next client know he was running a few minutes behind, James returned to stand in front of Treat.

"Give me your phone," he said, holding out his hand.

Treat fished it out of a pocket and handed it over. James quickly programmed his number into the phone, then texted himself so he had Treat's number as well. Handing the phone back, James leaned in and brushed one last kiss on Treat's full lips. "I'll call you, but it might be late."

"Okay," Treat said as he returned the phone to his pocket. "You'll call later."

With that, Treat slipped out of the locker room while James headed to his locker and changed.

****

The phone rang just as Treat was settling into bed at midnight. Grabbing his phone, he smiled at the caller identification. Sliding his finger across the screen, he rolled to his back as he lifted the phone to his ear.

"Hey," he said softly.

"Hi. Sorry it's so late."

James sounded tired, but then so was Treat. He had decided in the last few hours that if the man really did call, he was not going to let James hang up without making a date for something away from work. Even if it was just a workout over the weekend, he would make a date with James. He would then use that first date to start building a future with the man who, so far, fulfilled more than half of his list of what he was looking for in the man of his dreams.

Though he had been teased in the last few years

about being a slut for dating many men without committing to any, Treat was actually rather picky about the men he slept with. And though he had already jerked off twice since coming home just from the memory of their kiss, his cock was plumping up once more.

"How was your appointment?"

"Well, umm, that's why I'm calling. I was wondering if you could come get me?" James sounded odd, but then what did he know? He had only met the man that morning.

"Uh, well, Saint Michael's emergency room," James answered slowly, his words starting to slur slightly.

"Saint Michael's? What are you doing there?"

Treat heard the man sigh, and decided the answers didn't matter. He needed help, and if James was calling him, something else was going on. Treat rolled out of bed and grabbed the closest pair of sweats from the floor. Sometimes being a slob was a benefit.

"Never mind," James said before Treat could grab a t-shirt that he thought was clean. "I'll just let them check me in for the night."

"Hey, don't do that. I'll be happy to come get you. Give me about twenty minutes to get there, okay?"

"Really? Thanks," James's voice sounded like a two-ton weight had been lifted from his shoulders.

"Just chalk this up to a favor you owe me," Treat teased. "Or maybe I'll take repayment in kisses."

Treat knew he was pushing his luck, but James sounded like he might agree to anything if it got him out of the hospital emergency room. And the man did kiss really, really well.

"Umm, okay, that could work, I guess," James agreed. His voice and volume dropped when he added, "You're a good kisser."

"Okay, buddy. Hang on and I'll be there in a few," Treat slid into his truck. "I gotta hang up so I can drive now."

"Okay. See you soon."

The connection was cut, and Treat slid his phone into its holder on the dash. Starting the car, he pulled out and headed to the hospital across town. As he drove, his curiosity woke, so that by the time he pulled in and parked in the empty lot just outside the emergency room, he had a list of questions nearly as long as his arm for the man. He only hoped James was up to answering at least a few of them.

Walking through the sliding doors, Treat was shocked to see the waiting room empty. Crossing to the registration desk, he smiled at the woman dressed in navy blue scrubs sitting and looking half asleep.

"Good morning, sir. What's your emergency?" she asked as she turned to the computer on the desk without looking at him.

"I'm here to pick up James," Treat said, hoping she wouldn't ask for a full name because he was having a hard time remembering his own. Normally he was long asleep at this hour of the night.

"James? James Christian?" The woman tapped some more on her keyboard before looking up at him expectantly.

"Yeah, that sounds right," Treat said.

James Christian. He would have to remember that.

"And you are?"

He ignored her skeptical look and smiled brighter. "I'm his boyfriend, Treat Daniels. James called me to come pick him up."

"Uh-huh," the woman said. She did not seem happy with either his answer or his role in James's life.

No matter. It was what it was as long as James went along with his answers.

"Can I see him now, please?"

The woman gave a heavy sigh before pushing a button. "Go through that door and turn left at the first hall and go to the nurse's station. Someone can help you from there."

"Thank you," Treat said.

Turning, he headed to the door was that was still buzzing. Pulling on it, he followed the directions and turned left at the first cross hallway. He was surprised there were no patients in any of the beds he passed. At the nurses' station, he stopped and stared down the long desk. There was no one here, either. It was so quiet, that Treat began to feel like he had walked into the opening scene of some zombie movie.

Turning a circle, he saw no one in sight in any direction. "James?" he called softly.

"Treat? Is that you?" James's voice came from the hall to his left.

Treat headed in that direction. "Marco."

"Polo." James's response pulled him further down the hall.

In the last room down the hall, James sat on a gurney while a man in blue scrubs wrote on a computer tablet.

Except for the small square bandage taped to the left side of his forehead, a black eye that was swelling quickly, and a somewhat goofy expression on his face, James looked just as Treat remembered him from that morning.

"Treat, my man, my Tigger, you came," James said, sounding surprised.

"You call, I haul," Treat responded with a grin, amazed at James's attitude toward him. "What happened?"

James shrugged, and his expression turned guarded. "Just a little disagreement," he said cryptically. At that moment, he looked so mysterious Treat wanted to ruffle his feathers.

Suspecting he would get no more answers from the man, he turned to the man who wore a nametag that announced his name was Jimmy. "What's the scoop?"

"Apparently, Mr. Christian got between his employer and an empty bottle of whiskey."

"Client, doc. They're clients, not employers," James broke in.

"Calm down, big guy," Treat said as he patted a well-muscled shoulder.

He was shocked when it worked.

The surprises continued when James grabbed his hand and held it, not letting go as the nurse cleared his throat and continued.

"In any case, Mr. Christian suffered a head injury and though there are no breaks or obvious traumatic brain injuries, the medication we gave him had an unusually fast and stronger than usual effect. The doctor was afraid to send him home. Will you be okay taking him home and watching him for the next twenty-four to forty-eight hours?"

"Yeah, no problem," Treat answered automatically.

"You're so sweet," James said, leaning over and kissing Treat's cheek.

Problem was, he could not shift back to vertical without help. Treat took the man's leaning weight easily, then helped him straighten up again.

"Anything else I need to know?" Treat asked the attendant once more.

"If he starts vomiting or having unusual headache

or other symptoms, bring him back ASAP. He should see his primary care physician in a few days to make sure there's no lasting damage. It's all written in the notes, along with do's and don'ts and drug recommendations, though he refused to accept a prescription." The man handed Treat a packet of papers then looked at James once again. "Try to avoid bottles and bar fights in the future, Mr. Christian."

"Yeah, okay, but I wasn't looking for this one," James groused.

"Come on, big guy, let's get you home."

With Jimmy assisting him, Treat helped James into a wheelchair, though the injured man kept saying he was okay to walk. Once the nurse said it was hospital policy, James collapsed into the chair with a sigh. Once outside on the sidewalk, it took both of them to help the now completely loopy James into the passenger's seat of Treat's truck.

By the time Treat negotiated the big truck out of the maze of hospital roads and parking lots onto the street, James had slumped against the door and was snoring.

"Well, I guess that means you're coming home with me," Treat said, more to himself than to James.

In response, James snorted once and settled deeper into sleep.

Chapter Three

Pain.

Red hot, throbbing pain.

At first, James thought his head had been put in a vise. It took a few minutes before the pain localized to the upper left side of his face. Another minute and it was mainly his forehead and around his left eye that screamed with agony. Forcing his eyelids up, he frowned when his left one would not open fully.

Moving slowly, James turned his head just enough to make certain he was not in his room. The white-white walls and bright sunshine streaming in the double window were not familiar. His room was a smoky blue-gray with white trim and a single window.

A moment later, a warm weight around his middle that he had not realized was there lifted as the bed behind him shifted.

"Good morning, stud." The voice was familiar, but James could not place it. Thinking too hard caused the throbbing pain to amp up into white-hot, bring tears to his eyes level.

He didn't respond. He didn't move. He worked to breathe past the pain. Closing his eyes, he listened as whoever had shared the bed with him padded across the floor. A moment later, a door whooshed closed.

Once he knew he was alone, James eased over onto his back. As he did, an intense wave of nausea rolled through him. It wasn't just coming off the medication, he was so hungry he could eat the pillow under his head just to fill the hole in his belly. It took a moment, but when his stomach settled, he opened his right eye and worked on orienting himself once again

At the same time, he ran his hands down his body. A sigh of relief slipped out when he felt his boxer-briefs. Carefully pulling in a deep breath, he smelled lavender instead of the earthy scent of bodily fluids. Whatever he'd done the night before had not involved sex.

So what the hell had happened?

Slowly easing himself into a sitting position, James fought down another wave of nausea as he studied his surroundings. Wherever he was, it was the bedroom of a slob. There were clothes everywhere. The floor, the wide dresser with a television on top, and what he thought might be a chair in the corner were all covered with clothes. The only thing not hidden was the bed. He had a feeling that was only because he and whoever it was had slept in it.

Once he determined he had never before been to wherever this was, James tried to remember how he'd gotten here. But he could recall nothing. Before he dug too painfully deep into his memories, the bathroom door opened.

Treat Daniels strolled into the room wearing a pair of loose fitting boxers. Dark green with bright yellow smiley faces all over them, they made James smile just looking at them. Finding himself in the bed of the man he had met only yesterday, sent even more questions zipping painfully through James's brain.

"Where the hell am I?" he asked, his voice sleep rough and grumbly. He immediately regretted the volume when it, combined with the effort to speak, caused the pain in his head to spike past the moon. He winced and raised a hand to his head.

"And why am I here?" he whispered a moment later, once the pain eased back a bit.

Treat smiled as he sauntered toward the bed. "You're at my apartment. You're here because you fell asleep in my truck before telling me where you lived. Do you remember what happened last night?"

James tried to think, but the pain spiked again as he pulled up bits of memory. "There was a fight. Someone hit me with a bottle, and my client insisted I go to the emergency room. After that things get a little fuzzy to nonexistent."

"You called me from the emergency room and asked me to come get you," Treat said as he eased on the edge of the bed, their hips only a few inches apart.

His hair was sleep-ruffled, but otherwise Treat looked bright-eyed, bushy-tailed, and ready to tackle anything the world might toss his way.

James, on the other hand, felt like something big, heavy, and covered in spikes had rolled over him before backing up and rolling over him again.

"Where's my phone?"

If the sun was up and shining, he was running behind. The second day in a row. *Shit.*

"In your pants, I suspect. Let me go find them," Treat said before standing and heading out of the room.

Once he was alone, James slowly climbed out of bed and made his way to the bathroom. As he did, he fought a touch of dizziness and the unceasing pain that every step seemed to exacerbate. After relieving his overly full bladder, he stepped in front of the mirror where he gaped open-mouthed at the reflection staring back at him.

His left eye was swollen shut, and the area from his cheekbone up to the top of his forehead was one of those indescribable shades of black, blue, and purple that did not have a proper name on any color chart at the paint store. Or at least none James knew of. In the center of the bruise, just above his eyebrow, a thick, bright white square of gauze was held in place with paper tape.

Frowning caused more pain, so James forced his

face to relax. After carefully peeling the bandage off, he bent over the sink, and carefully splashed water on his face in the hopes of washing away more than just the slimy feel of a barely remembered bad night before. Once he felt more awake and alive, he dried his face on a hand towel Treat had thoughtfully left out.

The cut was an inch and a half long and started just at the top of his eyebrow and headed straight up toward his hairline. It must not have been too deep since the doctor had used superglue to close it instead of staples. Looking again at the face as a whole, he shrugged. This was as good as it was going to get.

Walking out of the bathroom, he found his clothes lying across the foot of the bed. His phone sat prominently in the center of his wrinkled black silk t-shirt. Looking at the little blue light that was blinking steadily, James sighed.

He wanted a day off.

He *needed* a day off.

After last night, he deserved a day or two off. He was injured, and his clients were just going to have to deal with it.

Swiping a finger across the phone screen, he sighed at the number of texts and voice messages waiting for his attention. Before he could open the first text and get to work, the phone was snatched out of his hand.

"No work today," Treat scolded. "I called the gym and told Rosie to reschedule all our appointments for the next two days."

James stared at the man in complete shock. "Why did you do that?" he asked, even as the thumping in his head grew stronger. He lifted one hand to his head in case it decided to fall off and roll across the floor.

"Because you need a couple days to heal," Treat said as he stepped close enough for their chests to bump.

Treat's skin felt warm against his own. "Once you're feeling better, I'm hoping to convince you to debauch me, among other things."

James felt like a movie character thrust into an alternate universe where his every wish came true. Because even if he only admitted it to himself, he really, really wanted to debauch Treat.

It was the man's next words that had him standing there chuckling instead of grabbing his clothes and storming out.

"I'm also hoping to help you pull that stick out of your ass before I convince you to help me prep for the season. But first, drink this and get back in bed."

Treat handed him a tall plastic cup full of orange-colored liquid.

James eyed it suspiciously, but when Treat did not go into detail of the contents, he sniffed the contents before taking a small sip. As he swallowed, he recognized the taste of the protein shake mix he had talked Dawg into selling at The Gym. Chugging the rest, he gave an indelicate burp once he finished.

Treat laughed as he took the cup back. James could not help but smile in response.

Once the laughter died away, James took a deep breath. As he released it on a sigh, the too-tense muscles across his shoulders and upper back released.

"Back in bed," Treat ordered as James reached for his clothes. "Rosie told me there was no way you would rest if I took you to your house, so you're staying here. I'll take you home tomorrow evening. That is, if you want to go," Treat's grin turned wicked and was accompanied by a wink that had James's cock twitching in response.

Treat's eyes boldly traced down his body as far his groin then rose again, this time looking determined as he took two steps back. "No. No, no, no. No sex. You're getting back in bed and resting. Sex will wait until later."

James wanted argue, but knew the man was right. "Okay."

Climbing back onto the bed, he settled. He felt like a little boy being put to bed by his mama when Treat tucked the blankets in around him. He half-expected the man to hand him a stuffed animal and kiss his forehead.

Instead, Treat planted a hand on either side of his shoulders, leaned close, and gently brushed his lips over James's. He straightened before the kiss turned from sweet to carnal.

"Go back to sleep," Treat ordered before bouncing out the room. He pulled the door closed behind him.

James took a deep breath, closed his eyes, and tried to go back to sleep. The only problem was, he was awake. While rest might be what the doctor prescribed, he was not ready to sleep again.

So, what should he do now?

****

Treat made it three steps down the hall before he stopped and leaned heavily against the wall. He could not believe his cock was hard again. After jacking to orgasm twice at the gym the day before, and once after putting James to bed, his cock should be limp, not hard as an iron spike. If he continued as he was, he would either jerk the damn thing off, or pass out from lack of blood in his head.

Neither sounded like much fun. But he needed to do something about the hard-on from hell, or it would be impossible to focus on anything else. And he needed to get some work done. He still had a long list of clients to inform about his move and talk into moving their membership and continue working with him at the new gym.

Walking into the kitchen, Treat tried to think past the need that clouded his thinking. But his cock refused to be ignored. It demanded satisfaction before he could focus on work.

Sliding one hand past the waistband of his boxers, Treat winced as his fingers brushed down the length of his cock. Lube. He needed lots of lube for this one. Spit on his hand was not going to cut it. Scanning the room, he smiled at the container on the counter next to the stove.

Butter. Sitting on the counter, it would provide more than adequate lubrication. It was within easy reach.

Perfect.

Shoving his shorts to his thighs, he reached for the butter. Popping the top, Treat dipped three fingers into the barely yellow substance. He ended up with way more than he needed, but it did not matter. Nothing mattered at that moment, except gaining relief so he could think past his need.

He slid his greasy fingers up the top side of his cock then down the bottom before wrapping his hand around the flesh. Closing his eyes, he sighed and leaned back against the counter as he began to slide his hand up and down the solid length.

"What the fuck?"

The question was whispered, but the words were just enough to startle Treat from his daydream of James and all the things he planned to do to the man. Forcing his eyelids up, he found James standing in the kitchen doorway in a t-shirt and boxer-briefs. The man looked stunned, though the impressive bulge at the front of his underwear told Treat he was not unaffected by the sight of Treat's self-indulgence.

Before Treat could react, James took the handful

of steps across the room. He was on his knees and licking the tip of Treat's cock before Treat's brain could catch up.

"Butter?" James asked, looking up at him.

"Uh-huh."

"Yummy." James pulled Treat's hand away from his cock. Parting his lips, he dove down Treat's length, taking him to the root.

"Ho—ly shi—t," Treat breathed as fire raced through his body at the wet heat that engulfed his dick.

How was he supposed to stay cool and in control when James began sucking hard as he slid up and down his fat cock? The man humming around his cock shoved Treat even closer to the edge of his orgasmic cliff.

Gritting his teeth, Treat balled his hands into fists and tried to focus on something other than James, but nothing slowed the orgasm balling up low in his belly. It would only take the smallest spark to set it off.

That spark came a moment later when James reached between his legs and cupped his sac. Treat sucked a sharp breath and held it as that simple, gentle touch lit the fine thread holding back his release. When the man rolled his balls then sucked his way down his length, Treat cried out as the battle was lost.

Unable to hold back any longer, he grabbed James's head and held on tight. His hips pushed forward several times, driving his cock even deeper. Finally, his seed exploded out of his balls, powered up the length of his cock, and burst out the tip in painfully strong waves. He had expected James to pull off. Treat was both surprised and pleased when the man swallowed down his seed.

When his cock stopped jerking and his semen stopped flowing, James licked Treat's flesh clean then held it gently in his mouth. Treat enjoyed the sensation for a moment, until orgasmic weakness washed through him. Too weak to remain on his feet, Treat slid down the cabinet he had been leaning against until his ass hit the floor. His legs extended on either side of James's still kneeling form.

Treat smiled at the man who sat back as he licked his lips. Unable to help himself, Treat leaned forward to kiss the man who had reduced him to a boneless pile of goo.

"Thank you," he whispered just before their lips met.

The kiss was long, but not frantic, though it was still filled with lips and teeth and tongues. He tasted the residue of his seed as it mixed with the flavor of the man in his arms. He liked the combination and could not wait to taste James's life essence.

Though he had just come, his cock began to stiffen once again. The need for air, and to move to a more comfortable venue finally drove them apart.

"Thank you," James said once they finally separated.

"I'd return the favor, but I'm not sure I can move. You've sucked me dry," Treat admitted.

He blinked in confusion when James began to chuckle. Had he said something funny?

He thought about what he had just said and could not help but join in as he recovered his strength. His body recovered enough to feel his fingers and toes.

As he opened his mouth to beg James to fuck him, James slowly rose then reached down and pulled him to his feet as well. Then the man winced and lifted a hand to his head.

"Come on, stud. You can fuck me later, when you don't look like your head is going to explode," Treat said as he took James's hand in his. Together they staggered out of the kitchen.

"Sounds like a plan to me," James whispered as they entered the bedroom.

Chapter Four

For an alpha-type male who was used to telling others what to do, it felt strange to give up control and allow someone else to be in charge. But that's what James found himself doing as he recuperated at Treat's apartment. The bouncy little man turned out to be quite the caregiver, and though he flirted and teased and turned James on like no one ever had before, he also kept his distance, refusing to finish what had been started in the kitchen that first morning.

When James was awake, they did talk about everything under the sun while playing cards, or putting puzzles together on Treat's laptop. James learned there was a competitive side to Treat and the man hated to lose, though his mood never changed. He remained happy, upbeat, and Tigger-like no matter what was going on.

Unfortunately, the same could not be said for James. As time passed, his mood darkened. He wanted, no needed, to do more than sit around while his muscles atrophied and his clients forgot about him. Sure, two days off was nothing. He'd taken that much time off before, but for some reason, this was different. He needed to get back to working out. Or he needed to get laid. Something to break the darkness that was wrapping itself around his soul.

"How's the head?" Treat asked on the evening of the second day as they were finishing up dinner of grilled chicken and broccoli, cauliflower, and snap pea salad.

"Better," James answered, surprised that the pain really had subsided to a barely there thumping instead of the nausea inducing throbbing it had been the day before. "Much better."

"Good," Treat said as he carried their dishes from

the living room to the kitchen. "Then it's time to deal with that stick up your ass."

James heard the clatter of glassware against metal, and then the rustle of fabric. A moment later, James sucked a breath when the man returned to the living room wearing nothing but a smile. Swallowing hard, he managed to say, "Uh, what do you mean?"

"I mean, that stick up your ass that seems to be growing by the hour because you're here recuperating and not at your place, or wherever you'd be right now, doing whatever it is you would normally be doing."

Treat crossed the room, his hard cock leading the way. Though his mouth watered to suck on that pole once more, James did not move. He was afraid to. His own cock, which had been hard most of the past two days, grew painfully hard and drained away all thoughts of saying no to anything this man was offering.

"Come on, big boy, let's go to bed," Treat said.

James did not fight when Treat grabbed his hand and pulled him to his feet. And he followed along without argument when Treat dragged him along to the bedroom. He even cooperated by pulling his t-shirt over his head while Treat pushed his pants down his legs.

And then they were both naked.

At that point, James wasn't sure what to do. Being the dominant male he was, he always, always topped. But for the last two days, he had allowed Treat to drive. Was the man expecting him to continue to follow along?

He relaxed when Treat stepped closer while wrapping one arm around James's middle. The other slid up his chest to wrap around the back of his neck "Don't worry, stud, you'll be in charge, but if you'd ever want to trade places, just let me know. I'm easy that way."

With that, Treat pulled his head down for a kiss

that would have blown James's socks off, if he had been wearing any. James parted his lips, but once their tongues touched in hungry lust, he took over. He hungrily explored every inch of Treat's mouth while allowing him to do the same.

When he felt his control beginning to shred, he began to shuffle them closer to the bed. As soon as he felt the mattress against the side of his leg, he turned them, then broke the kiss. Treat tried to follow then opened his mouth to argue, but James didn't give him the chance. Instead, he slid both hands to the man's chest and pushed.

He could not help the chuckle that rose at the look on Treat's face as he fell backward, landing on the bed. A moment later, the smaller man scrambled further up the mattress before flopping down on his back, his arms and legs spread wide.

"Debauch me, stud," he said with a giggle.

Though tempted to throw himself on top of the muscled man, James froze as practicality reared its oh-so-ugly head. "Supplies. We need supplies. Where?"

Treat lifted a hand and pointed to the nightstand to the left side of the bed without looking away from him. "Top drawer."

James hurried around the bed. It only took a moment to find what he needed. Tossing several condoms on the bed along with a bottle of slick, he slammed the drawer closed before climbing on the bed beside Treat. Pulling the smaller man back into his arms, he started the foreplay all over again.

He stroked fingertips over the mountains of Treat's muscles, licked lines over the valleys in between, marveling at the definition, the tone, and the fact that the man seemed to be nothing but muscle. He licked around and then over one beaded nipple and then the other, before tracing a line down the center of his body. He circled the man's bellybutton, then poked his tongue in, eliciting a giggle and then a moan.

Lifting his head for only a moment, he reached for the bottle of slick and a condom. His control was shredding fast, and he needed to get inside Treat before it completely unraveled.

Slicking up his fingers, he reached between Treat's powerful thighs and after rolling the man's balls, his attention moved to the pucker behind. A single finger slipped in, and after a moment, he added a second and then third. From Treat's restless movements on the bed, the man was more than ready for him, but seemed to be holding back.

"Tigger? What's wrong?" he murmured as he slid his fingers in and out with slowly increasing speed.

"Need. You. Now. Fuck me. Oh, God, fuck me now."

His answer was just what James was waiting for. Reaching for one of the pillows at the head of the bed, he tapped Treat's hip. "Lift."

The man's body arched up from the bed so fast and high, James was concerned he might have hurt something. But he seemed fine as he settled back down, his hips now resting on the pillow. As James moved to kneel between his legs, Treat pulled them up so it was clear sailing to find and enter his back hole.

James slid the head in, then paused as the muscles gripped him tight. The man seemed to be as toned here as he was everywhere else. Counting to twenty in his head, James began to push deeper and deeper until his balls were pressed against Treat's ass. Then he paused while Treat adjusted to his invasion, and he tried to hold back the orgasm that was already threatening to explode out of him.

Finally, Treat wiggled his entire body. "Move, dammit. Fuck me good."

His words, combined with the fiery look of lust in those bright green eyes ripped the last of James's control from him. Pulling back, he tried to keep the rhythm slow and easy, but though his intention was good, it was only a handful of strokes before he was power-driving into Treat, his orgasm growing closer and closer.

"I'm close. Oh, shit, I'm coming," Treat cried as his hips began to convulse.

"Thank fuck," James murmured.

He watched Treat's cock spasm, coating the man's belly and chest with his release. He then slammed deep once, twice, and on the third his body locked up. His seed pulsed out of his body, filling the condom that separated them in painfully pleasurable waves of release.

He maintained his strength long enough to ease his slowly deflating cock from Treat's hole before falling over onto the bed beside the man. He was unable to react when gentle hands stripped the condom from his cock before cleaning him up. A moment later, a warm body pressed into his side and Treat gently kissed his cheek.

The two men lay together, enjoying the afterglow as their breathing evened out and their bodies cooled.

James was almost asleep when Treat nuzzled his neck with his nose. "So, what do you think about coaching me for the upcoming season?"

****

Treat knew this probably wasn't the perfect moment to approach this subject, but he also knew that James's defenses were down and maybe he would agree. Their styles might be completely different, but Treat needed a coach who would take him the extra distance he needed to make it to nationals this year. His goal of earning his pro card in the next two years could only be realized if he had a winner behind him.

James was just the man for the job, even if he didn't realize it.

"You really want to talk about this now?" James tilted his head and looked down at him.

Treat lifted one shoulder in a half shrug. "Seems as good a time as any."

He held his breath as he waited.

James stared at the ceiling for so long, Treat was sure he was trying to talk himself out of his suggestion. Finally, the man took a deep breath, then released it a controlled manner that seemed almost a sigh, but wasn't. "All right, but we do things my way. No arguing, no cheating, no slacking off. Being together in bed will have no influence over how I treat you in the gym, understood?"

Treat wanted to jump to attention and salute, but instead nodded. "Yeah, sure, okay. Your way. Thank you."

James rolled and wrapped his arms around Treat's body, pulling the man up the bed until they were lip to lip again. "I'm not sure this is a good idea, but we'll see how it works out."

And then the talking ended and the loving began again.

By the time James finished with him, a long time later, Treat didn't have the energy to bounce out of bed and do the happy dance he wanted to do at having found a new coach. Instead, he curled up in James's arms and took a little nap with his man. After all, sleep was just as important as diet and exercise for an athlete's success.

****

"I am a lot older than you are," James said two weeks later.

Treat had just challenged him to add another plate

to the weights he had just finished lifting. He tried to stay in his logical brain even as Treat's hands tightened on his narrow hips. Shifting their hips back and forth, Treat rubbed their cocks together, the feel of which derailed his thinking as his cock began to make demands.

"Don't think you can keep up, old man? I'll ease up if you need me to," Treat said with that sexy, toothy grin that made him look like he had just uncovered all the secrets to sex. "But you do ten more reps, I'll give you a blowjob in the shower."

James knew Treat was playing him and shoved hard enough the man was forced to take a step back. With cooler air now permeating his shorts and cooling his fire-hot erection, he said. "I thought I was supposed to be coaching you, not the other way around, Tigger."

Taking a deep breath to center and focus on the moment at hand and not the prize at the end of the evening, James stepped into place. Without hesitation, he picked up the bar weighted down with iron plates at both ends and lifted it the requisite ten times. Though his body performed perfectly, his mind flashed to an image of Treat on his knees with water running over his pale, Irish skin. He swallowed to hold back the moan of hunger that threatened to emerge.

"And ten. You did it. Now that's your new limit," Treat said as James dropped the bar the last two inches onto its stand with a whoosh of breath.

"You owe me," James said as he swiped his hand over his face, wiping away the sweat that rolled down his face. A blowjob in the showers was going to feel so good.

"Don't worry, old man. I always pay my debts," Treat cooed as he stepped up and with a deep breath lifted the bar and quickly pushed out ten repetitions. "Want to try for another ten?"

James knew he had more than reached his limit with the last ten. And having finally overcome a dislocated shoulder from pushing too hard, he decided not to push any further. "Not unless you're willing to visit me in the hospital when my shoulders blow," he said, only half in jest.

Treat laughed as he sashayed to the next station in the circuit for working the back and shoulder muscles. "I'd rather keep you healthy so you can fuck me boneless later."

James followed, amazed at how easy it was to give in to Treat's sometimes goofy, almost always fun ideas, no matter how much trouble they might get into along the way. "Sounds like a plan to me."

Chapter Five

Treat watched from the front desk as a woman threw herself into James's arms with a squeal he could hear from across the noisy gym. His man caught her easily and returned her hug. Though they had ridden to work together after a night of hot, hot, hot sex, a stab of jealousy crashed through Treat's chest. He fought down the urge to march over and slap the plastic out of the skinny little bitch. Instead, he turned away and grabbed one of the protein bars from the display he had just finished stocking.

Rosie watched from her station behind the front desk. Her smirk told Treat they might not have been as discreet as they thought they'd been. But then, after a month of being a couple, Rosie was the only one who suspected that he and James were practically living together.

"Put that back," Rosie said. "You don't want to undo all your hard work with the competition only ten days away."

Treat looked from the unopened protein bar in his hands to the woman and blinked. She was right. Though he was always hungry these days, he could not let a cute little blonde female mess up what he and James had been working on since their second day together.

"I don't know how you do it," he said softly.

Rosie watched her man work with pretty, young women all day every day, and it never seemed to bother her. Not only that, but Dawg barely acknowledged her existence, except as an indispensable member of The Gym's staff.

Rose shrugged as her cheeks pinked up. She glanced toward the office where they could see Dawg on the phone. "I love him. I also know that, at the end of the day he'll be taking me to dinner and to the movies. The fact that he doesn't realize I'd give him any body part he might ever need doesn't matter."

Treat looked back to where James was now talking to the woman, a model he recognized as local weather girl Candi Bern. When she'd called, she had first begged for Dawg, who refused the job, then asked for James. She claimed that she needed to tone up for a new job.

As Treat watched them talking, he saw that Candi wasn't just here for the workout. She was after his man. She eased closer, and James would step back with a look in his direction. His expression screamed for Treat to rescue him, but Treat couldn't. As per the agreement they had made the morning after their first night together, they would not be caught kissing, touching, or doing anything else to out each other at work. So, instead of storming across the room and knocking the woman on her ass, Treat took a deep breath then turned and headed to the laundry room.

Let the man figure out how to get her to back off himself, though if this kind of behavior continued, he would demand they announce to the world they were a couple. For now, though, Treat had towels to fold.

****

"Come on, Jimmy, why are you acting all cold? I need you to whip me back into shape." Candi Bern gave a cute little pout as she ran a hand down his chest.

James had to admit, she certainly lived up to her name. She was an overly sweet Georgia peach, who burned through men like they were toilet paper. Grabbing her wrist, James looked across the room, hoping Treat would come to his rescue.

Instead, his man turned and walked away.

He was on his own.

"As I told you when you asked about getting back together, Candi, I'm with someone," James said.

He stepped back for what felt like the hundredth time. A moment later, she stepped closer, once again brushing her C-cup breasts against his shirt. This time her fingers, with their long red nails that looked like bloody claws, didn't stop at his waistline, but instead managed to slip under the elastic waistband of his sweatpants.

Grabbing the wrist, he forced her to step back as far his arms would allow. "I don't know who you think you are, lady, but just like a woman, when a man says no he means no. And from the look of you, you're not serious about working out tonight anyway."

Her glossy pink lips pooched out a little farther as she crossed her arms, which pushed the latest bit of artificial enhancement even further into prominence. "I don't know what you're talking about. I am here to work out. I need to be down a size in a month if I want to win the new Carla Christina modeling contract."

All James could do was shake his head. He had worked with her a couple times in the past when Dawg had been out of town, but could see why the man had handed her off to him when she called for this appointment. She thought big boobs and a sexy pout would get her anything she wanted. And, he now remembered a little too late, she had been wanting him back for a while.

In the past, before Treat had bounced into his life, James might have been tempted to take her up on her not so subtle offer to take their last session of the day out to dinner and further. But Treat *was* in his life now. Which meant Candi would never make the transition from client to something more.

Now he just had to get that across to Candi.

"If you were here to work out, and not flirt, you'd have your hair pulled back, your fake nails would be history, and you'd be dressed to sweat. Instead, you look like a Hooter's girl in your fuck-me heels and shiny Daisy Duke shorts," James said. "So, unless you have a change of clothes in that teeny sparkly bag of yours, we're through for today. Come back when you're serious about working out. Have a nice evening."

Before she could respond, James walked away. He headed to the front hall that led to the break room and laundry room. He wasn't ashamed to say the tiny woman concerned him, but for now, he needed to make sure Treat was okay.

He was peripherally aware that Candi stomped out as much as a one-hundred-pound girl in five-inch heels could stomp. He also knew she would be back. She wanted that modeling job and needed the kick-in-the-ass motivation he could provide. He'd just have to make sure that when she did return, she understood him in bed was never going to happen.

Just as he reached the laundry room door, Dawg and Rosie walked by, hand in hand. "Lock up tonight, okay?" Dawg asked.

"Sure thing, no problem," James said without hesitation.

This was perfect. The couple die-hard gym rats who were still in the building were finishing up their routines and would be gone within the next ten or fifteen minutes. Then he and Treat would have the place to themselves. Not only would they get their evening workouts in, but he hoped they would get their sexy on once they'd finished for the evening. His cock plumped at the thought of fucking Treat in this place where they spent most of their time.

Instead of continuing into the laundry room as

originally planned, James backtracked and headed to the locker room for supplies. After slipping several condoms and the small bottle of lube he had packed that morning for just this possibility, James returned to the gym. He followed the last person to the door and locked the doors. He turned out the lights in the front part of the building, but left on the ones in the back.

The room took on an almost sinister feel, but with the new clothing display in the center walkway, no one would be able to see them from the glass front doors. Now it was time to find Treat and put his hastily laid plan into action.

Easing the laundry room door open, James saw that Treat was nearly finished folding the freshly laundered towels that had been used during the day. Stacks of white towels covered the tops of both the washer and dryer. The man was currently pulling the last load from the dryer.

James groaned silently as his cock leapt to attention at the beautiful, round ass pointed in his direction. He debated whether he should kiss it or bite it, but decided fucking it would be more fun for both of them. He stepped into the room and allowed the door to swing closed behind him. He grabbed Treat's hips and ground his erection into the dip between his ass cheeks.

"She's just a client," he said softly when Treat stiffened.

"Then she needs to keep her claws off you before I decide to get bitchy," Treat said as he finished pulling towels from the dryer. He closed the door before straightening.

James slid his hands from Treat's hips up his body and around his chest, pulling the man back into his embrace. He grew nervous when Treat didn't relax, but remained as stiff as a toy soldier. "She knows that. She also knows that if she shows up again unprepared, I'll drop her as a client. That's the last thing she wants, especially since Dawg is about ready to drop her membership."

Treat relaxed just enough to give James hope he wasn't going to break off what they were building together.

At least until he asked, "Did you sleep with her? I mean … before."

Shit.

"Yes, Tigger, I did. Once. Last year when Dawg asked me to work with her. But it was only once, and it was long before you came into my life. No matter what she might think, it will never, ever, happen again."

He held his breath as Treat contemplated his words, not relaxing until his man turned around and melted into his arms. James was shocked to see the man's eyes were red and his cheeks were wet.

"You need to know I refuse to share. With anyone. And I'm not planning on letting you go any time soon, so deal with it."

James leaned down until they were nose to nose and eye to eye. "I don't cheat. And I don't share, either. We're a team. Together from now until we're old men chasing each other around the nursing home in our wheelchairs."

Treat blinked once before nodding slowly.

Before he could say another word, James tilted his head and closed the distance, kissing the man hard, fast, and with a dominance that he hoped got the seriousness of his statement across. Treat pushed closer and tightened his hold around James's body, making a possessive statement all his own.

Though tempted to fuck the man right here and now, James eased the kiss from carnal to gentle and sweet before breaking the lip-lock completely. "You have towels to finish folding and a workout to muscle through before we take that kiss to its obvious conclusion."

Treat blinked as his brain slowly caught up. "But…"

"No buts. Towels, workout, then hot, sweaty loving," James said, even as he took a step back before reaching down and shifting his iron hard cock into a more comfortable position.

Treat watched him with a slowly growing grin. Then he grabbed several of the still warm, unfolded towels and tossed them his way. James caught them automatically.

"Help me finish folding these damn things. I swear they're multiplying like rabbits as they sit here."

James folded the towels Treat had tossed at him, then left the man to finish up while he made sure the office had been shut down for the night.

****

Treat finished folding towels, but decided to hold off putting them away. He had learned on his second day working at The Gym that Rosie was only happy when she had something to grouse about. Having to put towels in the locker rooms was just enough, but not too much, to keep the woman's grumbly personality content.

And a happy Rosie meant a contented Dawg. Dawg was one man he had no desire to mess with. Ever. The gym owner was not only a retired Navy SEAL, he was also a former Mr. Universe. He still looked like he could bench press a Sherman Tank after eating small children for breakfast.

Turning out the light in the laundry room, Treat stepped into a gym transformed. Sure it was still a former grocery store, but the cold and imposing shiny white painted steel and black leather machines no longer glinted and gleamed in the overhead lights. Instead the place had become intimate and cozy.

Almost romantic.

His cock plumped up as he made his way to the back of the room where the leg machines waited for him. Switching his racing brain from work to working out took a few minutes, but by the time he had finished stretching, his mind was focused on the task at hand, pumping the iron he lusted after while being with the man he loved.

Treat froze.

Love? He loved James? Was that even possible?

His family had never been close and rarely, if ever, used that four-letter word when addressing one another. He wasn't sure he really knew what love was, much less how to love a man like James. The man was older and seemed to have his life together. He talked about his future in terms of five years down the road while Treat focused on just getting through the next ten days to his first show of the season.

He did know he wanted James in every way possible. He could not imagine his future without the man by his side. James pushed him when needed, cuddled him after a bad day, and helped him celebrate every little victory.

If that was love, then Treat had it bad.

He didn't even mind that James preferred to top him. He, Treat Daniels, was in love for, he hoped, the last time in his life. At that moment, bent in half as he stretched his lower back, everything was right with his world.

A sharp slap on his left ass cheek brought his wandering thoughts back to the task ahead of him. Pumping iron before pumping the man he loved. Because tonight, he was going to take the dominant role and show James how much he loved him.

"You waiting for an engraved invitation? Because I'm not sure there is such a thing," James said as he walked to the first machine they would be working on.

Treat straightened with a grin. Yes, he was going to fuck that stick out of his man's ass tonight, one way or another.

He settled belly down on the leather bench and moved so the backs of his ankles were pressed against the bar. He moved the pin that secured the weight to where he would begin and, with a deep breath to focus himself even further, got to work. James stood beside him, watching as he bent his knees up, pumping the weights ten times.

Trust. Another component of that love thing Treat had never experienced before. Turning his head to the right so he could see James's legs, he watched the man stand still as a statue. In an instant, he knew, he was indeed in L-O-V-E.

Opening his mouth, Treat froze. After several heartbeats he snapped his jaw shut again. He couldn't tell James. Not now. What if the man rejected him?

No, he would, somehow, wait until James declared his love first.

"Treat!" James voice was sharp.

Blinking, he looked at the man who looked like he had been trying to get Treat's attention for a while. "What?"

"You going to work out or just lie there grinning like a toothpaste model?"

"Oh, yeah. No, I'm gonna work out," Treat said.

Taking a deep breath, he forced his focus back so it extended only as far as the leg adductor machine and the muscles he was working. As soon as he finished ten

more repetitions, he rolled off the bench and James took
his place.

Chapter Six

By the time they finished the circuit of machines, Treat's clothes were sweat-soaked and the muscles of his lower body felt rubbery. Except his cock. That remained rock-hard and ready for action. His need to fuck James had grown over the past hour while he put his body through the routine he and three coaches had developed to keep his lower body in peak physical condition.

As he used the machines, he looked around, trying to decide where to spread James across so he could love on him. His bed was a fifteen-minute drive across town and James's was even farther. There was no way he could wait that long to slide his now rock-hard cock into James's sweet hole.

James looked hot, sweaty, and oh-so-sexy. The gleam in his eyes and the bulge pushing at the front of his leggings gave Treat hope that the man's thoughts were headed in the same direction as his. The man seemed to be up to something, and Treat hoped it meant hot, sweaty sex in their immediate future.

"So, what now?" Treat asked as he leaned heavily against a stepper machine.

"What do you want to happen now?" James responded with a sexy smirk that made Treat's cock twitch and drool just a little.

Turning his head, Treat scanned the gym. The adductor machine was closest, but was also in line with glass front doors. Looking farther away, he smiled when he found what he was looking for tucked back in the corner of the room.

"Come on," he said, grabbing James's hand and pulling him along with him.

James had turned the lights off in this area, leaving the corner in heavy shadows. The mirrored wall just a few feet away added a kinky twist to what he had in mind. When they reached the incline weight bench, he let go of James's hand. It only took a second to shift the bench so it sat parallel to the mirror.

When he looked at James, his man looked confused, but interested. "You planning on doing some lifting?"

"Not exactly," Treat said with a grin. He pulled the wet shirt over his head at the same time he toed off his sneakers. "Get naked. I plan on fucking you stupid."

James looked from him to the bench and back again. He tilted his head, then his grin grew until it was almost as big as Treat's. In the next few seconds, both men were naked.

"Shit," Treat realized he didn't have lube or a condom. "I forgot a condom."

"Here." James opened one hand and extended it in his direction.

Several packets of lube and a three-pack of condoms lay on his palm.

"Sweet."

Treat grabbed a condom and lube packet. After sheathing his cock, he turned and pulled James close. He needed to make sure James was all right with everything that was about to happen. The hug was awkward as their muscles didn't seem to fit well together, but the hot, hard, greedy mating of lips made up for it.

Their cocks brushed together, sending even more electricity thrumming through the air around them as they pushed even closer. Finally, Treat could hold back no longer.

Breaking the kiss, he turned James toward the high end of the bench. "Drape your sexy ass over this," he said.

Moving the forty-five-pound barbell to the floor

next to the mirror, Treat watched as James stepped up and bent over the back of the incline bench. Since it was a solid built bench instead of adjustable, there shouldn't be any problem of it collapsing under their combined weight.

James laid down, but immediately later pushed his upper body back up as he twisted to frown at Treat. "This thing smells like butt sweat."

Treat laughed and patted James's ass. "And how do you know what butt sweat smells like?"

James blinked, but didn't have an answer he was willing to share. Relaxing back down, he folded his arms against the leather to keep his face from touching it.

Instead of jumping in and getting busy, Treat took a moment to step back and look at all the sexy awesomeness that was his James. The golden skin, the bulging, rippling muscles, the man who was quickly coming to mean everything to him.

Moving to the side of the bench, Treat leaned down and started kissing damp skin. He kissed bulging muscles up and down his back, traced the valley of his spine down to the twin dimples just above the cleft that led to paradise. At the same time, he opened the packet of lube, and generously greased up his fingers. Though he was on the edge of sexual insanity, he was determined to take proper care of his man.

Stepping to the end of the bench, Treat took a moment to admire the ass cheeks and bulging leg muscles that had worked hard and were still pumped up. Leaning in, he kissed the peak of one globe and then the other. His fingers found the rosette that would lead him to paradise.

He slipped one finger in and out, greasing up the passage before adding a second finger. He took his time, sliding them in and out, curving them so his fingertips passed over the fleshy spot, earning a grunting moan with each stroke. At the same time, Treat continued to nibble on the salty-sweaty skin of his ass and lower back.

Adding a third finger once James had loosened enough for it caused the man to arch his back and come up off the bench. His long, low groan told Treat he was ready to move on to the main event. But Treat refused to hurt him, so he continued moving his fingers in and out until the muscles loosened just a bit more.

"Need you. Now," James fairly growled as he tried to fuck himself on Treat's fingers.

Treat was more than ready as well. Stepping onto the built-in metal ledge, he pulled his fingers from the hot hole, and replaced them with his cock a heartbeat later. Pressing forward slowly, he did not stop until his balls were pressed against James's. Their twin moans of satisfaction harmonized in the otherwise silent room.

Treat forced himself to remain still to give the other man a chance to adjust to his invasion. It was when the hips he held began to wiggle that Treat eased out until only the head of his cock remained before sliding forward and stopping once again. He grinned when James gave an animal-like growl.

"Stop messing around and fuck me already."

Treat began moving, trying to keep the pace slow and easy. It worked for about ten seconds before the hunger clawing at him demanded he move faster. The pace and strength of his sliding in and out of James's clutching heat increased. Turning his head, Treat watched the action in the mirror. It was almost as good as watching a porn film, but even better because he felt everything at the same time he watched it happening.

Dropping his gaze to where his body connected with James, he grinned as his cock pistoned in and out of James's body. His balls were pulling tight as the familiar tingle of his approaching orgasm began to skitter down his spine.

"I'm close, oh shit, I'm coming," James cried as his back arched up off the bench. He grunted with each shot of sperm that shot from his cock down to cover the bench.

Those words, and James's muscles clenching around him, were all it took for Treat's orgasm to explode. His hips locked as his balls pulled painfully tight. His seed jetted up the length of his cock to fill the condom that kept him and James as separate entities.

For a moment, Treat wished the latex barrier between them was gone. He wanted James to feel every drop of his life fluid as it filled him. Soon, he promised himself. As soon as they declared their love, he would demand they get tested so they could ditch the condoms.

Once his body unlocked, he eased his cock from James and stepped down from the bench. He took another step back before his legs gave out. He sat down, then sort of melted so he was sprawled out on the floor.

He watched as James worked his way off the bench and ended up on the floor as well. The man then crawled over and collapsed right next to Treat. A moment later, he lifted an arm and leg over Treat's body before snuggling him even closer.

"We need to go home," Treat said a few minutes later as his stomach began to rumble.

"Yeah, we don't want your stomach breaking out and attacking anyone," James responded in his dry, no-nonsense tone.

It took a moment for Treat to realize the man was joking. The man was always so serious that sometimes Treat was tempted to tickle him just to see him laugh. He was so beautiful when he laughed.

Neither man thought of the mess they had left

behind until they walked in the next morning to a grumpier than usual Rosie. "You two, follow me," she said, tossing a spray bottle at James and two rags at Treat.

They dropped their bags and the cooler at the front desk and did as Rosie commanded. She marched down the main aisle, then veered off and continued straight to the weight bench. "Since you two closed last night I am going to assume this mess belongs to you. Clean it up," she said, pointing to the bench where streaks of semen had dried. As she walked away, she finished with, "And figure out how to get the stench of a bordello out of the air while you're at it."

Treat looked at James, and both men burst into laughter, which continued until they had finished cleaning the bench, moving it back into place, and returning the barbell to its rightful place.

****

James groaned when his phone sang out with yet another text message just a second before the alarm went off. Candi had been blowing up his phone, since she'd shown up the afternoon after their first meeting dressed appropriately and ready to sweat. It had been a week, and instead of accepting that she had no chance with him, she seemed to take his relationship with Treat as some sort of whacked out personal challenge.

She seemed to have decided James had become more than just her thrice-a-week trainer. She now texted, or called, about everything. At first, it was for advice about extra exercise she should do between their sessions. Then she started in with questions about her diet. Two days ago, she had begun asking his opinion on clothes, sending him pictures of her wearing scanty, clingy dresses, shirts, and even lingerie.

Reaching for the phone, he punched the

appropriate buttons to pull up the three texts that had come through in the last minute. Yep, it was her. Reading the messages, he typed a quick answer before hitting send, hoping this would end the texts. He had only been responding to the ones pertinent to his position as her trainer. The others he had deleted without responding.

"Her, again?"

Treat sat up, rubbing the sleep from his eyes with one hand while ruffling his curly hair with the other. He looked so cute, James was tempted to drag him back down to start the morning with some down-and-dirty sex. Except then they would be late to work, if they made it there at all.

Instead of reaching for his man, James rolled out of bed. "Yes, she's begging to move her session to this morning instead of this afternoon. I told her if she could be there at five-forty-five I'd work her in. You're just doing cardio and don't need me watching the clock for that."

Treat shrugged as stretched his arms above his head. His rippling, flexing muscles made it hard for James to climb out of bed, but he forced himself to. "Okay, I'll share you today. But she lays a finger on you, I'm ripping her arm off and beating her with it."

James chuckled before he said, "I'll pass along that message."

The two men went through their morning routine of dressing and packing food and water for the day using a big cooler. They gulped down a pre-workout protein shake full of vitamins, minerals, and other all natural goodies that would help their muscles grow as they burned up whatever fat was left on their bodies. With the show only a few days away, they were both as ready as they could be.

James was surprised to see Candi's red Camaro

was already in the parking lot when they arrived at work at two minutes to five. Treat carried the cooler, and James carried both their gym bags as they crossed the parking lot. Treat remained quiet and very un-Tigger like as the blonde woman climbed out of her car.

"James?" she said, her voice a strange combination of whining and begging.

"Five-forty-five, Candi, and you'd better be ready to sweat," James said.

He didn't slow his pace, or look in her direction. Out of the corner of his eyes, he did see her give Treat a narrow-eyed, considering look.

Was she seriously thinking of taking his man on?

James focused on the man by his side. "Don't," he said so softly Treat was the only one who heard him.

"Don't what?"

"Don't think about going after her. She's not worth it, and could do some serious damage to your future," James said as he opened the front door.

"I'm not," Treat said, though his tone was hardly convincing.

James only hoped he wouldn't have to referee a fight this morning. That was one sure way for Treat to flush his career. Dawg would not only kick him to the curb, he would be blackballed from working at every gym in town. And that would probably extend to the state because the competitive bodybuilding world was a small one. And that was the last thing his lover needed.

"I know you've reached the foggy, brain-dead stage of prepping, but keep your cool, okay?"

Treat nodded, then turned to head to the small room the staff had claimed as their own. It had a refrigerator for their food, a table, and couple of chairs for meals. There was also a couch, but Treat avoided that at all costs.

His third day of work Treat had made the mistake of sitting down on the couch for a few minutes. He ended up sleeping for an hour. Not cool when his coworkers decided it would be fun to toss a blanket over him then take selfies with "the snoring mountain". The teasing had continued until just the day before when someone else had been caught napping.

James went to the locker room and stowed their gear in his locker because it was bigger than Treat's and would hold both bags. Then he returned to the main gym where Treat waited beside one of the elliptical machines.

"So what are you waiting for? The show's in three days. Get your ass moving," James ordered with a grin as he stepped onto the machine he always used, just three down from Treat.

With his man beside him, James started walking his warm-up, his thoughts going to how good his life was.

Chapter Seven

Life sucked big, stinky, hairy donkey balls, Treat thought the next evening as he watched James once again correct Candi's form as she posed in the mirror. The woman had become his worst nightmare, but he couldn't say anything to James.

Not without looking like a jealous idiot.

Though James had assured him she was just a client, Treat knew Candi had in mind something more up close and personal than just working out. How James didn't see it was a head-scratcher because she wasn't subtle in her actions. Treat wanted to step in and scratch her eyes out, but that would be completely unprofessional.

Every time she got around Treat with James out of earshot, she would whisper sweet nasties about replacing him as the man's number one client, in bed and out. So far, Treat had not responded, but it was only a matter of time.

"Come on, Tigger, let's go home," James said, twenty minutes later. He sounded almost as tired as Treat felt. The competition was in two days, and tonight they both needed a good night's sleep. Tomorrow would be spent away from the gym doing a bodybuilder's version of a spa day. Manis, pedis, and spray tans were on the agenda in preparation for check-in tomorrow evening. The competition started early Saturday morning and went all day, for those who made it through the preliminary rounds.

"What about her?" Treat asked. He nodded toward where Candi was preening in front of one of the mirrors wearing clothes that barely covered her bits and pieces. A handful of men openly ogled her from various points around the room.

"What about her?"

"Is it safe to leave her here alone? Those guys are looking pretty predatory," Treat said.

James's gaze swept the room. "I'm so tired and hungry, I don't care anymore. Her session with me is over. I don't know why she's still hanging around."

"She hasn't gotten everything she wants yet," Treat said, feeling more than a little snotty. He blinked when James frowned at him, looking confused. "You can't be that naïve, James. She wants you back in her bed, and she's not going to give up until you're there."

This time it was James who blinked. Then he began chuckling. "You're jealous," he said as he pushed through the front door and out into the parking lot. "Oh my God, you're jealous of that bit of feminine fluff."

Treat fought down the need to scream out the truth that of course he was jealous. Instead of answering, he stalked to his truck, his jaw clenched shut and his teeth grinding. James followed, still chuckling until he climbed into the passenger's seat.

"I'm sorry, but you're cute when you're jealous. You have to know she's never going to get anywhere with me. I love you, Tigger. Only you."

Treat froze at the words he'd been dying to hear. All at once his emotions boomeranged from the depths of despair at not holding his man's heart, to the highest joy at knowing the man who held his heart loved him back.

Slowly turning in his seat, he blinked back tears that appeared out of nowhere. "I love you, too. So very much."

Leaning forward, he met James halfway over the center console in a deep, wet, thorough kiss that curled his toes and stiffened his cock. He put everything he couldn't say into that kiss. For someone who in the past didn't do emotions, it was a kiss filled with meaning. It was several minutes after they parted before he was able to start the truck and drive them back to his place. There was still a lot to do in preparation for tomorrow's show.

Treat didn't know what to say on the drive home, and from the silence on his side of the truck's cab, James seemed just as stunned. It wasn't until they were behind the locked door of his apartment that Treat finally spoke, asking the only thing that came to mind.

"Will you shave my back tonight?"

Treat watched as James blinked. His lips twisted in a smirk before he nodded. "Only if you'll shave mine."

"After we eat?" Treat said when his stomach clenched, reminding him of the real reason they had come home.

James nodded again. "After we eat, Tigger. Then, we'll clean up and pack for tomorrow. What time is your appointment to get tanned?"

Treat frowned as he tried to remember. "Ummm," he said.

Going to the refrigerator, he looked at the schedule of events he and James had written out. "Mine is at two, and you're scheduled for two-thirty. Registration is at six. I'm supposed to wear my posing thong to sign in."

James nodded as he typed on his phone.

Once he finished, Treat pulled their dinners out of the refrigerator and put them in the microwave to heat up. Two minutes later, he carried the bowls to the table. "Dinner," he said with a grin.

James handed him a blender cup before taking his seat across the table. "Drink up, then eat," he said, lifting his own cup in a silent toast.

Once they finished eating, Treat followed James's lead in cleaning up. He was proud of the fact that he was getting better at picking up after himself, putting dirty dishes in the dishwasher, piling dirty clothes in front of the washing machine instead of tossing them on the floor to be dealt with later.

Carrying his bag into the laundry room he frowned. The pile in front of the washing machine was threatening to take over the entire laundry room. Adding today's clothes would surely send it toppling over.

Instead of tossing the damp clothes to the pile, he opened the washing machine and tossed them inside. Then he began loading other clothes until the machine was full. Adding detergent, he closed the lid and turned the machine on. He would come back after they showered and move the clothes to the dryer so he could start a second load.

Pulling the door close behind him, he smiled. James really was a good influence on him. If only he could say same about his impact on James, but the man was still rather rigid and unbending, except after a good session of loving. Then he was warm and snuggly, but that effect didn't last as long as Treat would wish for.

He hoped his winning the competition would help take some of the starch out of James's personality so he could relax and smile more easily. Then he would figure out how to get the man to agree to finally go public with their relationship. Then maybe Candi would back off and find a boyfriend of her own.

****

James stroked his fingertips down Treat's back, checking to make sure the skin was smooth and he had not missed any hairs. For a man as furry as a chipmunk, it had taken some time to shave away all the hair on his back while he had shaved the rest of his body clean. Fortunately, the apartment came with a tankless water heater so they wouldn't run out of hot water before he was as smooth as Treat now was.

Stroking one finger all the way down Treat's spine and down between the cheeks of his ass, James smiled as the man arched into his touch. Treat then moaned as the pad of James's finger rubbed over his puckered anal star. Leaning down, he kissed Treat's shoulder, then licked his way up to his earlobe, which he pulled between his lips to nibble on.

Reaching over, he pumped hair conditioning onto his fingers. Sliding two fingers into Treat to the first joint, he released Treat's ear. "Here or bed?" he asked, his voice rough as he offered his young lover a choice. If it was up to him, he would bend the man over here and shove into the hot channel that was currently massaging his fingers.

"Here. Now." Treat grunted as he stepped back far enough from the shower wall to bend forward. With his head pressed against the wall, he reached back with both hands and pulled the rounded globes of his ass apart.

James added conditioner and a third finger to Treat's ass, needing to take care of his lover so there was no pain before adding a third finger to his ass. Fucking his fingers in and out several times, he only hoped his man meant what he'd said.

Touching all that beautiful skin had left him starving to be one with his man. Since they'd been tested several weeks ago, it was hard to keep from fucking the man all day every day.

After another moment of sliding and twisting his fingers in Treat's chute, James pulled them free. He quickly slicked up his cock and then fit the head in place. One sharp thrust of his hips had his cock half buried in Treat's body. Shifting his feet for better balance, James pushed forward again until his pelvis pressed tight against those gorgeous ass cheeks he was having a hard time not marking up with love bites.

He held his breath as he leaned over and pressed his chest to Treat's back. He was so close to coming he needed a few seconds to rein himself back in. He counted to ten in order to give Treat a chance to adjust to the intrusion, and to push his orgasm back long enough to bring his man some pleasure.

"Fuck me, dammit." Treat pushed up until his body was more of a forty-five-degree angle. Planting his hands against the wall, the smaller man began to shift his hips back and forth, fucking himself on his cock.

Well, that answered the question of whether Treat was ready for him to move, James mused as he wrapped his hands around the man's water-slicked hips. Holding them steady, he began to push in and out. As usual when it came to loving on his man, control was not to be found.

"James. Oh shit, I'm coming," Treat cried out after a half dozen strokes, most of which pressed on his prostate.

Those were just the words James had been waiting for. Pushing deeper once, then again, on the third stroke he growled out his own release as his cock twitched with each jet of seed that left his body and filled Treat's.

Pushing on his man, James leaned them both heavily against the wall, the warm water still running over them. It took several minutes to find the strength to pull from his lover's body and clean up.

Once they were squeaky clean again, James turned off the water while Treat reached for the towels waiting on the counter. They dried each other and then, with arms wrapped around each other, staggered to the bedroom and fell into bed. James had just enough energy left to pull the covers up over their bodies. Treat was already snoring by the time he snuggled up against his back. In less than a minute, he joined Treat in Morpheus's embrace.

Chapter Eight

For the first time in the ten years he had been competing as a bodybuilder, Treat felt uncomfortable during the check-in process. Not that he wasn't prepared—he was. With James's help and coaching the last few weeks, he felt he was better prepared than ever before. Treat was ready to take on the competition and leave them eating his dust. He would win today, and win big.

The uneasy feeling came as he watched James strip off his t-shirt and sweatpants. Treat didn't want anyone else looking at his man. At least for the classic physique competition, which James was registered for, he didn't have to wear the slinky, satiny, shiny micro-bikini, showing off nearly every inch of his body. Like the one like Treat wore under his sweats.

"Weigh in and then bring your form back to me, please." The woman behind the table handed him back his paperwork.

There were two dozen people in the room, but Treat saw only James as he stepped off the scale, a big smile on his face as he looked around for him. When their eyes met, Treat winked. That smile meant only one thing, his man's weight was far enough below the cutoff between heavyweight and super-heavyweight that he would be competing at the top of his class. Now if only Treat got the same happy news.

"Leave your stuff here," an older man said, demanding Treat's attention. The man, who looked like he should be competing himself, pointed to the table beside Treat. "Strip down and step on the scale, please."

Treat quickly did as ordered. He dropped his flip-flops, black t-shirt, and sweats on the table then stepped on the electronic scale. He held his breath as the little red lines went 'round and 'round, assessing his weight. When the numbers flashed, he wanted to crow with happiness. Like James, he had qualified for the heavyweight class with room to spare.

After redressing, he returned his paperwork to the lady at the desk, received his competitor's package and informed of when he needed to be back for the prejudging round. Once he was finished, he turned around and found James waiting for him.

"All done?" he asked, wishing he could throw himself into his man's arms for a celebratory hug.

James nodded, looking a little uncertain. Without a word, he turned and walked out of the room where the registration was begin held. Treat hurried after him. James didn't stop until he had entered the men's room just off the hotel lobby where the competition was being held.

"James, what's wro—oomph," Treat said, the air exploding from his lungs as his man twirled and pushed him back against the door to the hall.

His lips slammed over Treat's, demanding entry, which he gladly allowed. It was in that instant that Treat realized he wasn't the only one affected by having his man nearly naked in a room full of strangers. And he *was* wearing the teeny-weeny bikini that left next to nothing to the imagination. James's black boy shorts at least covered his full ass and hips.

"I've got two hours. Let's go upstairs and mess up the sheets."

Treat grinned at his suggestion. He had three hours before he had to be on stage. Getting freaky would certainly keep his nerves under control. He just hoped his tan could hold up to the sweating he was certain would be taking place. "Okay."

James had already reserved a hotel room for last

night and tonight before they had gotten together because, as he explained, it was more convenient to stay here instead of trying to run back and forth several times over the weekend. An added benefit was by staying at the hotel their newly sprayed on tans wouldn't mess up the sheets at either man's apartment. Plus, after the finals tonight, win or lose, they would have a celebratory meal at the BBQ place next door and afterwards just have to go upstairs, instead of drive back home again.

After another kiss that had Treat's costume squeezing tighter and tighter, the two men broke apart and left the restroom. As much as he wanted to hold James's hand, it was not permitted.

And that sucked.

Once this weekend was over, he was going to demand they sit down and discuss their relationship and why they were hiding it from the world. It wasn't like he was going to fuck his man in the middle of The Gym, but it would be nice to be able to touch him in public without worrying about how James was going to react.

They weren't the only ones in the elevator, though Treat didn't think the older couple, dressed nearly matching black suits, had anything to do with their competition. But, from the way James kept a good foot of space between them, Treat knew any attempt to touch him would not be welcomed.

He waited until they were safely inside their room before grabbing James's hand and pulling him in for a big, chest pressing, arms entangled bear hug without the hair. When James's arms came around him and tightened, pulling him even closer, the little knot of negative emotion Treat couldn't put a name on melted away.

Surprised by the shift in his heart, Treat was happy to just stand there wrapped in his lover's arms for the rest of the day. To hell with the competition. To hell with everything outside this room. Resting his forehead on James's shoulder, he blinked rapidly to keep what felt like tears at bay.

Why was he crying? Was this part of the emotion thing that he'd successfully avoided all his life?

"This feels good," James whispered in his ear just before he brushed a kiss over the side of his head.

"Uh-huh," Treat said in agreement, his throat squeezing tight and making it hard to swallow, much less talk.

Treat adjusted his arms to pull James closer until all that separated them was the soft cotton of their t-shirts. Taking a deep breath, he sighed and relaxed even further into the embrace. It just felt so damn good.

James seemed content to just stand there hugging as well. At least he didn't move away, or try to take anything further.

Treat lost track of how long they stood there. It was a cell phone ringing across the room that finally broke them apart. Someone was calling James. Treat had a damn good idea who it was, but reluctantly released the man in his arms. By the time he reached the phone, the ringing had stopped, but started again as he picked it up.

Sliding his finger, James frowned at the number on the screen before putting the phone to his hear. "Hello?"

Treat tuned out the conversation as he turned on the television and found a music station. He then stepped into the bathroom to make sure his hair was holding up okay. Normally he didn't care how his messy, curly hair looked, but onstage today, how his hair behaved was just as important as how the rest of him looked under the dark brown fake tan.

****

James hung up the phone after repeating himself three times that no, he was not leaving the competition to meet Candi for lunch.

"She needs a new trainer. A female who won't put up with her antics," Treat said as he stepped back into the room.

"Yes, she does. You know anyone who might be interested in taking her on?" James said, turning off the phone and laying it on the table.

"Sorry, I don't. But between us we should be able to find someone. Tomorrow," Treat said.

James smiled as his man slowly crossed the room, his hips swaying to the music. "Tomorrow," he agreed easily. Today's focus was the competition.

As Treat continued dancing, James could not help but chuckle as the next song began. It was the same song that had been playing when he had first met the man in the locker room at The Gym. "Strip," he said, all at once wanting to see his man dance again.

Treat listened to the music and grinned. In seconds, his shirt and sweatpants were off. James could only watch and drool as the man turned away from him, then pushed his bikini shorts down and danced his way out of them.

Watching the smaller man move only added to the heat that was burning in James's heart, and loins. He needed to be inside his man. He quickly stripped off his own clothes as Treat continued dancing, his hips swaying back and forth and up down. His muscles rippled in the lights they had left on, contracting and relaxing and calling for James to stroke and lick each and every one.

But licking was off limits. So was bending his man over the bed and fucking him until they were both limp noodles.

Instead, James began dancing, moving closer as

he matched his moves to Treat's. A new song began, a slow, bluesy instrumental that brought to mind swirling ceiling fans and long, lazy nights of loving.

Wrapping his arms around his man, James pulled him back to lean against him, then slid his hand down the center of his body and wrapped his hand around Treat's cock. Treat's moan as he began to slowly slide his hand up and down the man's erection showed James that he approved.

He kept his grip loose and his moves slow and easy, as they danced together. The next song was faster, but their side to side swaying remained unhurried. He could not help his smile of approval when Treat stopped swaying side to side and began a back and forth motion instead.

"Let it loose," James said. The man's movements grew stronger, then less coordinated as his cock grew thicker in his grip. "Give it to me."

It wasn't but a moment later that Treat punched his cock through James's now tighter grip several times before arching his back and crying out. His spunk arced through the air to land in a puddle on the carpet just outside the bathroom door.

"Shit," Treat breathed as he leaned his full weight back against James, "that was so good."

Before James could think of a response, the man in his arms spun around and dropped to his knees. In the next instant, his mouth had taken James's cock to the base and was sucking and swallowing on it like it was the end of times and he needed one last taste of sperm.

The heat, the wet, the massaging, combined with the joy of getting Treat off just moments before had him racing to the finish faster than James would have liked. But there was no holding back. He was too close.

Laying his hands on Treat's shoulders, James

held on as his body began to move of its only accord, his hips punching forward to fill Treat's mouth with every centimeter that made him a man.

Treat took it like a pro, sucking and swabbing and swallowing everything down when his load erupted like a jet. Once he finished coming, James had just enough energy to stagger the two steps to the bed before collapsing in a boneless heap. As Treat crawled up beside him, he only hoped he could pull himself together again in time to make to the prejudging.

"I love you, my Tigger," he said as he pulled Treat into his arms.

"I love you, too, stud."

Chapter Nine

Treat paced the contestant prep room, trying not to freak out. James had received an emergency call just after they'd finished their preliminary rounds, but that had been hours ago. The final round of competition had begun, and not only had James not called to let him know what was going on, he wasn't answering Treat's calls or texts either.

"Classic physique competitors to the stage."

Treat shook his head at the announcement as he headed to the backstage area. Maybe James had gotten back and was there already. Surely he wouldn't miss this after all the months of preparation and sacrifice he'd gone through.

Treat found a place out of the way where he could see the stage, and watched as the finalists in the various weight classes went through their routines. When the heavyweight class was called, James did not make an appearance. The judges waited an extra two minutes before striking his name from the competition and continuing on.

"You're not supposed to be out here yet," one of the officials touched his arm. "You need to go back to the green room."

"Yeah, okay," Treat said as he turned away from the stage. There wasn't anything to see anyway.

The rest of the evening passed in a blur. His first-place win in his class, and overall, barely sank in because the one man he had hoped to celebrate with was still MIA. Not sure what else to do, Treat gathered his belongings and headed upstairs. He needed a snack before he took a long, hot shower.

Then, if he still hadn't heard from James, he would get some BBQ and take it back to his apartment.

Staying in the hotel tonight without James with him just didn't feel right. Hell, right now he wasn't sure if he should be angry the man had disappeared, or worried that something had happened to him to keep him from coming back.

By the time he'd showered and dressed, there was still no word. No text, no message, and when his called it went straight to voicemail.

"Well, hell, stud, where the fuck are you?"

Not sure what else to do, he packed up his stuff. It was a waste of money, but he wasn't going to stay here alone when he had a bed only twenty minutes away. Looking at James's bag, he made an executive decision. It only took two minutes to pack his stuff as well. Then, carrying both their bags, he left the room. Dropping the key at the front desk, he left a message for James in the hopes the man showed up.

After calling a taxi for a ride home, he went to his favorite BBQ joint and walked out a few minutes later with several pounds of meat, potatoes in every form they offered, and a family size container of banana pudding. Whether or not James showed up, he would be feasting tonight.

The cab was pulling in as he stepped out of the restaurant, juggling the two bags of food and the duffel-bags of clothes that didn't want to stay hanging from his shoulders. In the taxi, he texted James and updated him on where he was and that he had gotten food already. Maybe, if he was lucky, James would be at home waiting for him with a really good reason why he'd blown off the rest of the competition.

Treat hoped.

But James wasn't.

By Sunday morning when he still had not heard from the man who claimed to love him, Treat had moved from worry through brokenhearted to being pissed, but not sure what he was supposed to do about it. Except for practically living together, loving hard and frequently, and James coaching him, there really wasn't much tying them together. Especially since James refused to acknowledge they were a couple anywhere except in their apartment.

Treat just wasn't sure how to react when James walked in Sunday night as if he'd just run to the grocery store for dinner.

****

James was exhausted, hungry, and his skin itched. All he wanted was a two-pound steak with all the trimmings, a shower, and his bed, preferably with Treat in his arms. Entering the apartment he now shared with his Tigger, wondered if he had enough gas left in his tank to get the shower before getting dinner.

"Where the hell have you been?" Treat's voice sounded equal parts accusatory, worried, and heartbroken.

Not sure how to respond, James stopped. "I had an emergency to deal with," he said.

"And you couldn't call?"

"I'm sorry. My phone died. I didn't have a charger with me. And without my phone, I didn't know your number."

He watched Treat turn that information over. It took a moment, during which his man looked like he was either going to cry or burst into a rage. James wasn't sure which one would have been easier to deal with.

Finally Treat said, "So, where the fuck were you?"

"The hospital. Candi…"

"Say no more." Treat cut him off. "If she's the reason you missed the finals, missed me winning the overall, and have out of touch for more than a day, I don't want to hear it. If she has that kind of power over you, maybe you shouldn't be here. Maybe we shouldn't be together."

Before James's tired, hunger-fogged brain could come up with a response, Treat stormed into the bedroom and slammed the door. All thoughts of his bodily needs and discomfort evaporated as James stared at the door that stood between him and the man who held his heart, his entire heart, in the palm of his hand.

Yes, Candi had taken up a lot of his time lately, a lot more than any of his other clients, but she was just that, a client, while Treat Daniels was so much more. His Tigger had become his whole world. Now all he had to do was figure out a way to convince his man.

Crossing the room caused his clothes to shift on his body, reminding him that he still needed a shower. Opening the door, he left it open and crossed to where Treat was sitting on the bed, staring out the window. Sitting down beside the man, James took his hand and held it between both of his.

"Candi overdosed yesterday morning. For some reason, she had me listed in her phone as her emergency contact. It took until this morning to get her phone company to override her security so we could contact her family. I stayed with her until her parents arrived this afternoon."

"Oh, my God," Treat whispered, clearly shocked by James's confession. "I'm so sorry. I thought…"

"Shhh, Tigger, it's all right. I should have figured out how to get a message to you, but by the time I thought to call the hotel, you had left," James said. "I'm not making excuses, but for a while they weren't sure if she was going to live or die. I didn't want her to be alone if she didn't make it."

James was stunned when Treat leaned over and rested his head on his shoulder. "I'm sorry. I'm such a shithead. I should have known it was something big to pull and keep you away. Forgive me?"

"Only if you'll forgive me for not having your digits memorized," James turned his head and brushed a kiss over the top of his man's head.

Taking a deep breath, Treat said confidently, "Yes, I forgive you. We'll memorize each other's numbers, after."

"After?"

"After you get a shower and we get you something to eat. 'Cause, buddy, I gotta tell you, you stink and look like you're about to fall over."

James chuckled as Treat pulled away. "Yeah, I do. And people at the hospital were looking at me like I was a creature from outer space."

Treat smirked as he stood up then turned and pulled James to his feet as well. "I'll just bet they did. Come on, I'll wash your backside. And there's leftovers from my celebratory meal we can heat up."

"So how did you do?" James asked as he pulled off his clothes, leaving a trail across the bedroom and into the bathroom.

"First place class, and first place overall," Treat said, sounding so casual about the wins.

"That's great, Tigger," James said, his heart glowing with pride at his man's accomplishment. "You're going to have to keep up the good work and maybe you'll earn your pro card by the end of the season."

Treat shrugged as he finished undressing. "Maybe. There was a photographer who gave me her card, asked if I would be interested in doing some modeling work. She takes pictures for those romance book covers."

James grabbed his man and forced him to do a little happy dance with him right there in the bathroom. "That's amazing. I hope you told her yes," he said.

"I told her I'd have to think about it, and talk to my manager," Treat said with a playful glint in his eyes. "So what do you say, manager? Want to see this body on a book cover?"

James pressed their bodies together as best he could as he said, "You know I do, that is, if it's something you're interested in doing. Don't do it just because I think you'd look smoking hot on a cover or anything."

"Don't worry, I won't. Now get in there and scrub up." Treat stepped back and pushed him toward the shower. "Then we can talk about you maybe being on a cover with me."

****

On Wednesday morning, James was quieter than normal, but then they both were. Candi's parents had called to let him know that the damage from Candi's suicide attempt was just too extensive and they had decided to withdraw life support. He had gone with James to the hospital so the man could say good-bye.

Then Treat had taken James home and held him as they mourned her loss. For no matter how much Treat wasn't a fan of the woman, he hated suicide even more. There was nothing in this lifetime that couldn't be worked through.

Entering The Gym, he headed to the break room and transferred their food into the refrigerator. After Sunday night's feast, they had agreed to keep on their diet routines so they were ready for the next show, which was only a couple weeks away.

Walking into the gym, he hesitated when he saw

the staff, and all the early morning gym rats gathered in a circle in the center of the room.

"What's going on?" he asked as he approached, wondering if he had missed a notice about a meeting.

The circle broke and became a horseshoe with James standing in the middle, looking a little nervous though his eyes glinted with excitement. That made Treat's stomach clench. Something was definitely going on.

He froze when James stepped up, wrapped his arms around him and pulled him in for a hug. The man was trembling, though Treat couldn't tell if it was from anxiety or excitement. Tilting his head back, Treat looked up into James's dark eyes.

"Treat Daniels, my Tigger, my man. After getting burned bad by clients I dated in the past, I made the decision to keep my love life out of the gym and far away from my work. Then you danced your way into my life and heart. I can't keep my personal life and professional life separate any longer. I ask, here and now, in front of these witnesses, God, and all His angels, will you marry me, train with me, and continue lusting after the iron with me as long as we both can lift?"

Treat felt his eyes go wide as he processed the question. This was a hell of a way to come out of the closet to their friends and coworkers. But he was all for anything that would announce them as a couple to the world.

As he began to bounce with happiness, he threw his arms around James and hugged his man tight. "Yes, James Christian, I will."

The End

KEELY JAKES

EVERNIGHT PUBLISHING ®

www.evernightpublishing.com